This book belongs to

LJ LK O D4 O

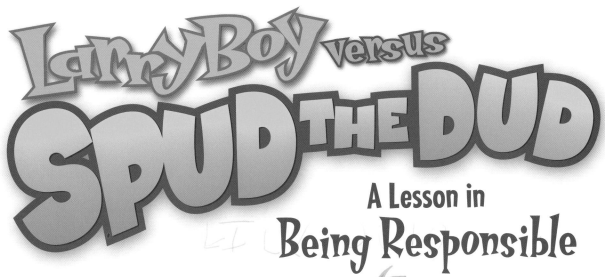

LarryBoy versus SPUD THE DUD

A Lesson in Being Responsible

by
Doug Peterson

Illustrated by
Tom Bancroft and **Rob Corley**
Colored by Jon Conkling

SCHOLASTIC INC.

New York Toronto London Auckland Sydney
Mexico City New Delhi Hong Kong Buenos Aires

He's slower than a speeding snail—lazier than a drowsy dog—unable to lift dirty clothes from a bedroom floor! Look! In the hammock—it's a slug! It's a bump on a log! No, it's—*Spud the Dud!*

6

Yes, it's Spud the Dud.
He's a strange potato who
came to Bumblyburg with powers
far less than those of normal citizens.
     It had all started one day when he arrived
at the home of Junior Asparagus . . .

"I don't wanna walk the dog!" Junior whined. "Can't I do it later?"
"But Wonder-Pup is *your* dog," said Junior's mom. "She's your responsibility—your duty. When we got Wonder-Pup, you agreed to walk and feed her."

That was true. But that was then. Now, Junior just thought
that Wonder-Pup was a great big bother.

"Junior, it's important to do small jobs when you're young," said
Mom Asparagus. "It'll get you ready for big responsibilities when
you're older."

Junior moaned as he trudged outside with the dog.

Suddenly Junior heard a voice say, "You're right. That dog *is* a big bother."

"Who said that?" Junior asked, whirling around.

Junior was stunned to see a strange potato in his yard. The potato was lying in a hammock, wearing an old, tattered superhero suit.

Junior asked again, "Who are you?"

"The name is Spud the Dud, and I think you're right," said the potato. "Why walk the dog when you can lie around eating cheesy puffs? How would you like to join me in my quest to rid the world of 'big bother' responsibilities? You'll even get to wear a spiffy superhero sidekick suit." The potato added, "What d'you think?"

"I think I would really like to be a superhero," Junior said. He was thrilled when Spud the Dud gave him his own special superhero sidekick suit to wear!

Little did Junior know that it was all a trick! The moment he put on the sidekick suit, Spud pulled out a remote control. He pointed it at Junior and pushed a button.

CLICK!

The remote controlled Junior's suit. It made him move. But worst of all, it made Junior do everything for Spud the Dud!

"HA-HA-HA-HA!" Spud cackled. (He had been first in his class in sinister laughing.) "Junior, you are in my power! Soon all the children of Bumblyburg will be serving *me*!" Spud clicked the remote and snarled, "Get me more cheesy puffs!"

"Help!" cried Junior in shock.

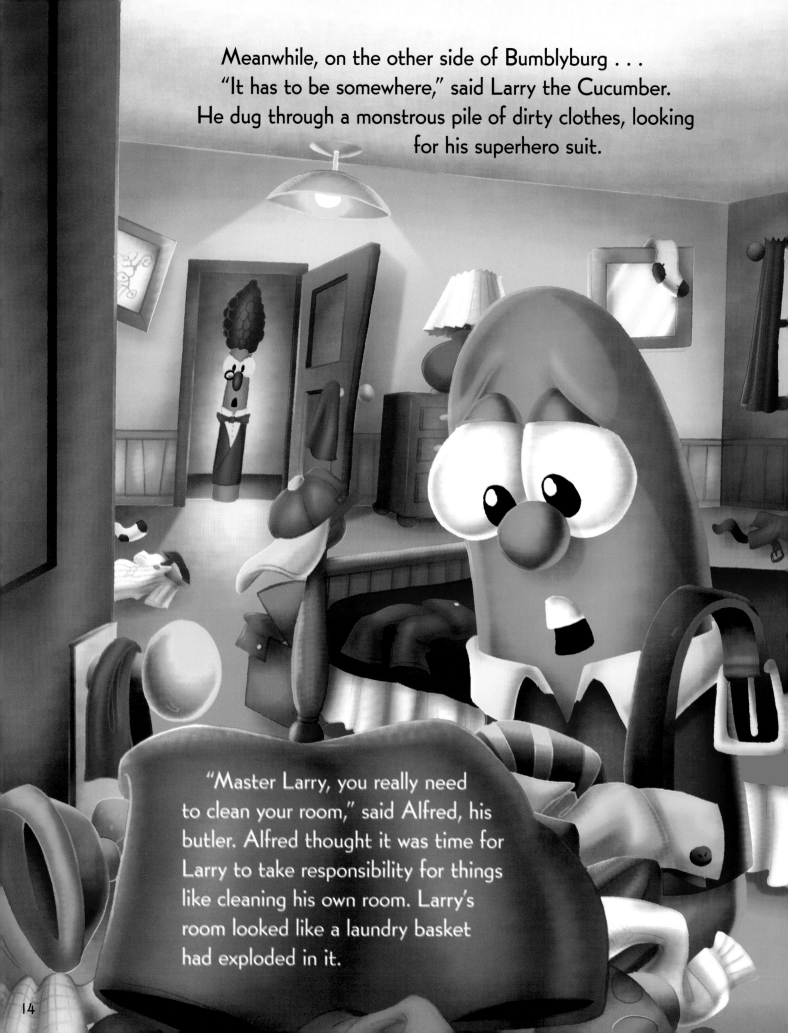

Meanwhile, on the other side of Bumblyburg . . .
"It has to be somewhere," said Larry the Cucumber.
He dug through a monstrous pile of dirty clothes, looking
for his superhero suit.

"Master Larry, you really need
to clean your room," said Alfred, his
butler. Alfred thought it was time for
Larry to take responsibility for things
like cleaning his own room. Larry's
room looked like a laundry basket
had exploded in it.

RINGGGG!

Alfred picked up the phone. It was Mayor Blueberry, and there was big trouble in Bumblyburg.

"Quick, Master Larry!" Alfred said. "Spud the Dud is taking control of the city's children!"

"But I can't find my suit!" Larry shouted. He finally dug up an old, torn superhero suit and said, "I guess this old thing will have to do."

So Larry dashed into his closet and came out as the plunger-headed hero—LarryBoy!

LarryBoy raced to Junior's neighborhood. The superhero couldn't believe his eyes. Spud the Dud was using his remote to control kids. He was making them do chores, scratch his head, and fan him with palm branches.

"Let those kids go free, you stuffed potato!" LarryBoy declared.

"Try to make me, PickleBoy!" scowled the lazy tater.

"Then take this!" LarryBoy fired one of his plungers. The pitiful plunger from the old suit wobbled around before coming back and hitting LarryBoy squarely in the face.

THOMP!

"Now I know why I stopped using this old suit," LarryBoy said. But with a plunger stuck on his face, it sounded more like, "Nahow Ino why Istopd singing dis moldy shoot."

THONK!

Yanking the plunger loose, LarryBoy tried again. This time the plunger shot straight and hit Spud's hammock squarely.

"It's working!" LarryBoy shouted, as he fired his second plunger at the potato.

But the second plunger struck the back
of a passing train instead!
"It *isn't* working!" cried LarryBoy.

The racing train yanked LarryBoy into the air, dragging him and Spud behind it. As LarryBoy and Spud whipped wildly around the bend, the LarryBoy Cell Phone rang. It was Alfred.

"Make it fast, Alfred!" LarryBoy yelled. "I'm kind of busy being pulled to my doom because my plunger is stuck to a train. Besides, you're using up all my minutes."

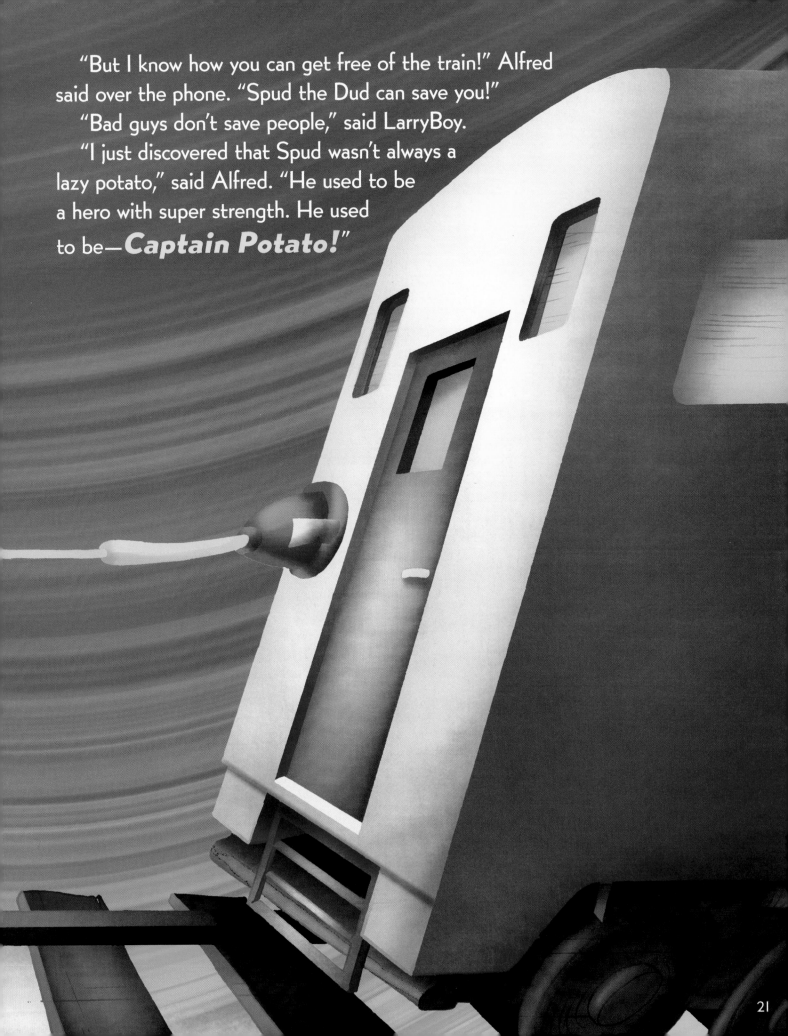

"But I know how you can get free of the train!" Alfred said over the phone. "Spud the Dud can save you!"

"Bad guys don't save people," said LarryBoy.

"I just discovered that Spud wasn't always a lazy potato," said Alfred. "He used to be a hero with super strength. He used to be—**Captain Potato!**"

LarryBoy couldn't believe his ears. Neither could Spud when LarryBoy tried to tell him that he was once Captain Potato.

"If I'm Captain Potato, then I would have a cape," Spud said. "Where's my cape?"

"Good point," said LarryBoy.

But that's when LarryBoy spotted it. Underneath a big splotch of cheese on Spud's hammock, LarryBoy saw the letters *CP—Captain Potato!*

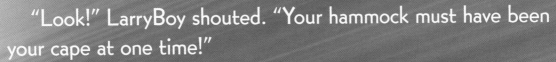

"Look!" LarryBoy shouted. "Your hammock must have been your cape at one time!"

Spud was shocked, but then it all started to come back to him. Maybe he did have more power than he thought. Yes, deep down, he wasn't always a lazy tater.

With a burst of super energy, Spud pulled his hammock apart and put on his cape. It's true! He **was** Captain Potato! He was stronger than a racing train! In fact, Captain Potato was so strong that he brought the train to a screeching stop.

He had saved the day.
Right then and there, he
knew he would never go
back to being that lazy
old Spud the Dud again.
He was a new potato.
He now *knew* he was—
Captain Potato!

The next morning, while Junior happily walked his dog, he glanced up. Look! Up in the sky—it's a bird! It's a badly dressed burrito! No, it's **Captain Potato!**

Captain Potato had learned that using his super powers was a lot more fun than being lazy. He took all the sidekick suits back and threw them and the remote control away so that the kids of Bumblyburg were free again! Junior had learned that being lazy isn't as much fun as it looks and that real happiness comes from being responsible and doing what you're supposed to do, not just what you want to do.

As for LarryBoy—he was right behind Captain Potato, swinging from tree to tree with his plunger ears. "Hey, this old suit works after all!" LarryBoy shouted in delight. "Maybe I can—"

POP!

KA-BASH!

"Oops." After LarryBoy's plunger popped loose, he crashed into a garbage can.

"Maybe I'd better clean up my room after all," LarryBoy muttered from inside the can.

People who refuse to work want
things and get nothing. But the
longings of people who work hard
are completely satisfied.
Proverbs 13:4